PRINCESS HEART

Princess Harper Gets HAPPY

by Molly Martin

pictures by Mélanie Florian

PICTURE WINDOW BOOKS
a capstone imprint

I'm Princess Harper Hannah Marie Easton, and I am happy.

Happiness makes my smile shine,
and my eyes sparkle.

It even makes my curls bouncier!

When I'm happy,
I feel like singing.

I feel like running.

I feel like dancing.

I feel like skipping.

I am happy walking
through my kingdom.

I wave and smile
at everyone I see.

I am happy helping
my sister.

I share my clothes
and toys with her.

I am happy spending time with friends.

I invite them over for tea and cookies.

I am even happy being alone.
I go for a walk. I listen to the birds sing.
I watch the flowers dance.

I know that whenever a princess sees someone who is sad or upset, she should help them.

I want everyone to feel
as wonderful as I do,
so I try to make other
people happy, too.

I love to share my happiness with the entire kingdom.

Doesn't that make you feel happy, too?

Princess Heart books are published by Picture Window Books
A Capstone Imprint
1710 Roe Crest Drive
North Mankato, Minnesota 56003
www.capstoneyoungreaders.com

Library of Congress Cataloging-in-Publication Data
Martin, Molly, 1979-
Princess Harper gets happy / by Molly Martin ; illustrated by Melanie Florian.
p. cm. -- (Princess heart)
Summary: Princess Harper is a happy girl and she wants
everyone in the kingdom to share in her happiness.
ISBN 978-1-4048-7852-5 (library binding) -- ISBN 978-1-4048-8108-2 (paper over board)
1. Happiness--Juvenile fiction. 2. Emotions--Juvenile fiction. 3. Princesses--Juvenile
fiction. [1. Happiness--Fiction. 2. Emotions--Fiction. 3. Princesses--Fiction.]
I. Florian, Melanie, ill. II. Title.

PZ7.M364128Prl 2013
813.6--dc23

2012026420

Image credits: Shutterstock/Pushkin (cover background)
Shutterstock/Kalenik Hanna (end sheets pattern)

Printed in the United States of America in Brainerd, Minnesota.
092012   006938BANGS13

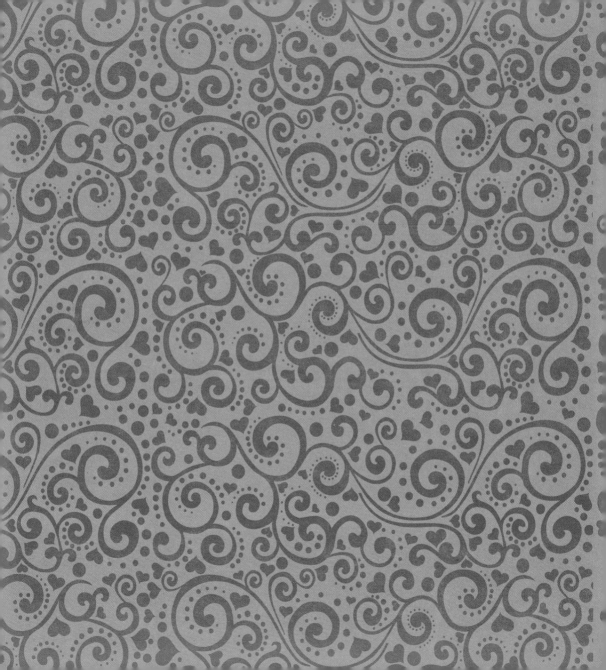